LET'S EXPLORE
EARTH

by Walt K. Moon

SCHOLASTIC INC.

Note to Educators:

Throughout this book, you'll find critical thinking questions. These can be used to engage young readers in thinking critically about the topic and in using the text and photos to do so.

Text copyright © 2018 by Lerner Publishing Group, Inc.
All rights reserved. Published by Scholastic Inc., 557 Broadway, New York, NY 10012, by arrangement with Lerner Publications Company, a division of Lerner Publishing Group, Inc.
Printed in the U.S.A.

ISBN-13: 978-1-338-26944-4
ISBN-10: 1-338-26944-5

3 4 5 6 7 8 9 10   40   26 25 24 23 22 21 20 19

Table of Contents

Planet Earth

Earth is a planet.

It is where we live.

It is part of our solar system.

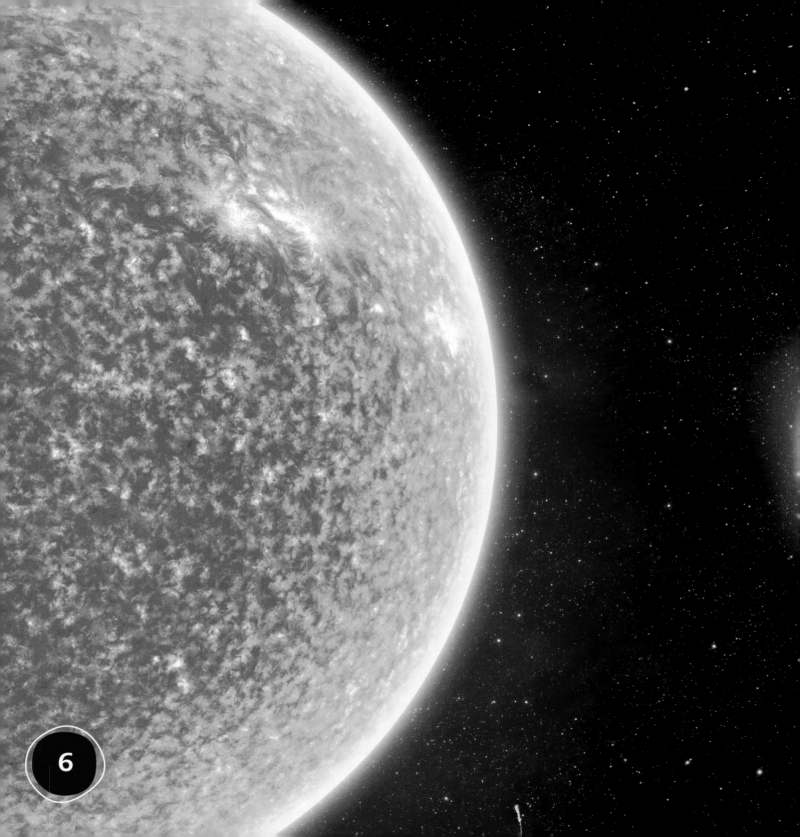

Earth moves around

the sun.

It takes 365 days to go

around one time.

This is one year.

Earth spins.

It takes twenty-four hours to spin

around one time.

This is one day.

When part of Earth is in light,

the other part is in shadow.

The other part is in the sun.

This makes day and night.

Is Earth in a shadow during the day or night?

Earth is tilted.

Some parts get more

sunlight than others.

This makes seasons.

Which season is the coldest? Which is the warmest?

12

Earth has pieces of land.

These are called continents.

There are seven continents

on Earth.

Can you name any of the continents?

Earth has a lot of water.

Continents are separated by oceans.

ocean

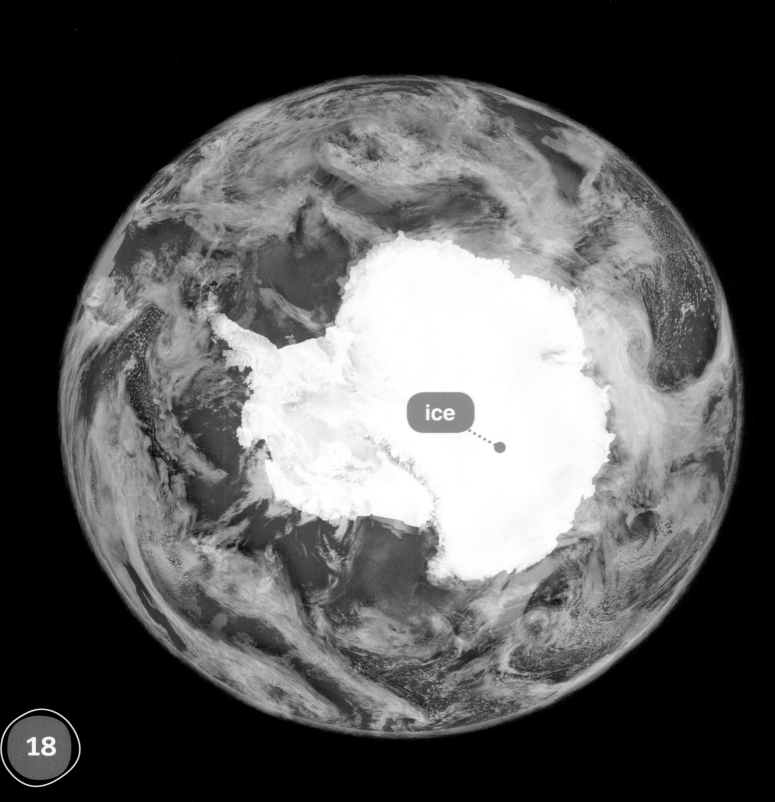

Some parts of Earth are very cold.

They are covered in ice.

Earth has many plants

and animals.

Some live on land.

Some live in the ocean.

Earth

Where Is Earth?

Picture Glossary

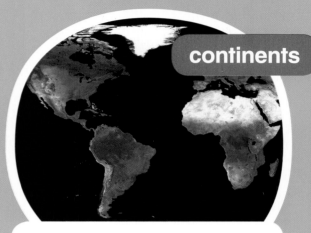

continents

the seven large pieces of land on Earth

oceans

the large bodies of water that cover most of Earth

seasons

the four parts of the year

solar system

the sun and the bodies that move around it

Read More

Hughes, Tom. *Day and Night.* New York: Enslow Publishing, 2017.

Moon, Walt K. *Let's Explore the Sun.* Minneapolis: Lerner Publications, 2018.

Storad, Conrad J. *Earth Is Tilting!* Vero Beach, FL: Rourke Publishing, 2012.

Index

Photo Credits

The images in this book are used with the permission of: © Juergen Faelchle/Shutterstock.com, pp. 4–5; © Aphelleon/Shutterstock.com, pp. 6–7; © solarseven/Shutterstock.com, p. 9; © Egyptian Studio/Shutterstock.com, p. 10; © Bas Meelker/Shutterstock.com, pp. 12–13; © pio3/Shutterstock.com, pp. 14–15, 23 (top left); © Photobank gallery/Shutterstock.com, p. 17; © Harvepino/Shutterstock.com, p. 18; © Andrey Armyagov/Shutterstock.com, pp. 20–21; © Christos Georghiou/Shutterstock.com, pp. 22, 23 (bottom right); © Shelli Jensen/Shutterstock.com, p 23 (bottom left); © EpicStockMedia/Shutterstock.com, p. 23 (top right).

Front Cover: © leonello/iStock.com.